ARABELLA'S JOURNEY

FROM SHADOW TO SUNSHINE

VRITTI AVICHAL

This book is dedicated

To my Grandparents,

who taught me power of words.

Contents

Foreword

I have read the story of Arabella. I am in awe of this young author Kum.Vritti, age 13 years. It surprises me how strong her imagination is and the way she has conveyed her thoughts through her book. Turning every page of this book made me even more grateful towards life.

Arabella has known little beyond the harsh realities of life in an orphanage, where each day is a struggle for survival and hope seems a distant dream. Surrounded by challenging conditions and devoid of familial love, Arabella's resilience is her only companion. Her life takes an unexpected turn when she is adopted by a renowned and compassionate doctor couple who offer her the warmth and security of a true home.

In her new environment, Arabella discovers the joys of being part of a loving family. Her adoptive parents, with their unwavering support and kindness, help her heal from the scars of her past. However, the transition is not without its challenges. At her school, Arabella becomes the target of bullying, facing hostility and cruelty from some of her peers.

Determined not to let her bullies define her, Arabella draws strength from her new family and resolves to confront her tormentors. Through courage, resilience, and the support of her parents, she addresses the bullying head-on, fostering understanding and standing up for herself and others who suffer in silence.

As she navigates these trials, Arabella blossoms into a confident and empowered teenage girl. Her journey is one of self-discovery, healing and the transformative power of love. By overcoming adversity and forging her own path, Arabella not only triumph over her bullies but also inspires those around her.

In the end, Arabella's story is one of hope and redemption. She lives happily ever after, secure in the love of her adoptive parents and proud of the person she has become. "Arabella's journey from Shadow to Sunshine" is a poignant tale that celebrates the resilience of the human spirit and the life-changing impact of compassion and familial love.

While working as a Judge, I had occasion to visit the child care homes, orphanage homes. Though I visited many times to see whether boys/girls like Arabella get quality food, clothes, clean toilets, timely medical treatment, I missed the emotional bonding to be made with the children. After reading this book I realized it. There was more to do for the orphan children by understanding their emotional, mental condition. This book has shown me how to understand them. Mere visit to them is not sufficient. In future, when I would again visit orphanage I will be able to interact with children, in better way.

Arabella is a must read for young children as well as adults to understand the importance of loving family as well as appreciate and enjoy every moment in life, to do something meaningful for the orphan children. I congratulate Kumari Vritti and her parents. I wish Kumari

Vritti all the best for future and to write many more books by which the children, youngsters, citizens, NGO's will get inspiration to work for orphan children and senior citizens.

Jaywant C Yadav

Assistant Sessions Judge, Nagpur

Foreword

In a world that can often feel cold and unforgiving, Vritti Avichal's Arabella's Journey from Shadow to Sunshine is a refreshing reminder of the power of the human spirit to persevere through even the darkest of circumstances. This poignant tale follows the life of Arabella, an orphaned teenage girl navigating a harsh reality that would shake even the most steadfast of souls.

Yet what makes Arabella's story so profoundly moving is not merely the adversities she faces, but the grace, courage and compassion with which she chooses to face them. As we journey alongside her, experiencing the depths of her loneliness and sadness, we also bear witness to the kindling of an unwavering inner strength- a light that guides her towards hope, love and the warmth of true friendship.

Vritti Avichal deftly reminds us that life's greatest joys are not found in material wealth or grandiose achievements, but rather in the simple yet precious moments that fill our days- a sunny afternoon, a kind word shared between friends, the comfort of an embrace. It is a celebration of the small things that make our existence radiate with meaning and beauty.

At its core, this book is an impassioned call to meet the harsh realities of our world not with resignation or bitterness, but with an open heart filled with love, kindness and the unshakeable belief that good will ultimately prevail. For even in the seemingly darkest of nights, the human capacity for hope can never be extinguished.

Arabella's Journey is a story that will linger long after the final page is turned – an indelible reminder that by embracing all that life offers with patience, courage and compassion, we too can emerge from the shadow and bask in the radiant warmth of the sunshine.

Sr. Vasantha Kommareddy

Principal

Villa Theresa High School

Gopalrao Deshmukh Marg,

Mumbai-400026.

Dear Reader,

Read this book at your own pace - whether it's one chapter a day, two chapters a day, or the entire book in a single sitting. It's completely your choice. It would be nice if you could sit in peace, as this is a book where the reader needs to immerse themselves in the protagonist's life and feel each emotion which our heroine, Arabella, felt in her journey of life.

A special tip: Stay wide awake and lighthearted to contemplate your reading with a cup of coffee. This dose of caffeine will come to your rescue to help you complete this book faster.

Author's Note:

I began writing this book when I started to unfold the power of words. I sat with my laptop and an idea, and the rest of the story came to my mind. I always dreamt that someday I would write a book, and in that process, I navigated all the feelings I had and found a voice that helped me to write it. Our minds are most liberal; in no way could we encapsulate our thoughts. Instead, they allow the reader to introspect and relate to the emotions Arabella experienced.

When I look back at this story, I feel as if I have lived the life of Arabella and felt just the same as if I had faced similar situations. To me, this is much more than just a compilation of 11 chapters; it is an amalgamation of emotions.

Vritti Avichal

Preface

Writing "Arabella's Journey from Shadow to Sunshine " has been a deeply rewarding experience for me. The story is about a teenage orphan girl who faces many challenges in a tough world before finally finding comfort in a loving family. It highlights themes of resilience, love, and hope.

As Helen Keller once said, "Although the world is full of suffering, it is also full of the overcoming of it."

This story aims to inspire readers to believe in a brighter future, even when the present seems difficult. There's a beautiful anecdote from "To Kill a Mockingbird" by Harper Lee where Atticus Finch tells Scout, "You never really understand a person until you consider things from his point of view... until you climb into his skin and walk around in it."

Thank you for joining Arabella on her journey. I hope her story touches your heart and encourages you to make a positive difference in your life as well as life of others.

Prologue

'Arabella's journey from shadow to sunshine' is a story of change, showing how strong people can be and how love and care can make a big difference. It's about facing tough times, discovering your strengths and believing that every tough situation can turn into something better, full of hope and joy.

In the words of William Wordsworth:

"The best portion of a good man's life :

His little, nameless, unremembered acts

Of kindness and love."

Life

I am Arabella. I am thirteen years old. As you read my story, I want you to be my friend and good listener. As I narrate my story, I am reliving each moment of my life again. Instead of being depressed, I would like you to count the blessings God has bestowed upon you.

Being an orphan living in an orphanage, I was always envious of kids who had their parents to pamper them. I was forced to stay in an orphanage under the supervision of Mrs.Pinto. She was a short, stout, fair and avaricious woman. All the kids in the orphanage were neglected. We were not allowed to play with each other and were forced to do daily chores to escape punishments. Errors were not accepted at all. Her extravagant lifestyle was funded by government donations intended to maintain the orphanage.

I heard from my friends that she found me at the orphanage's door. I had been abandoned by my parents when I was just nine months old. She was the one who gave me shelter, food and clothing to survive. I'm not attempting to imply that I thought she could take the place of my parents. I was happy to have atleast a roof over my head because of her.

Unlike the kids born with a silver spoon who were served five meals a day, my friends and I had to settle for one meal, which was a plain roti with watery dal and a vegetable, which I swear we wouldn't like, as it didn't have any taste. We had either potato or bottle-guard as a vegetable in the meal. Our daily chores comprised of mopping the orphanage, cleaning the washrooms, washing utensils, chopping vegetables, helping in cooking, and most importantly, never making Mrs.Pinto angry.

Despite all that, everyone in the orphanage was happy as we had Mr.Pinto with us. He was Mrs.Pinto's husband. He was very kind and compassionate but Mrs.Pinto always overpowered him as she came from a rich family background. She would fight with Mr.Pinto and would make his life miserable. Unlike Mrs.Pinto, he loved us and always took care of us. He was disheartened as he never wanted any one of us to be her slave. He would also share the same meal with us, which was dry roti in watery dal as he considered us his children.

From a very young age, my perspective of life was completely different. I was filled with anger, jealousy, and most importantly, the desire for freedom from this matrix. I never wanted to be a weak minded person. At night, before going to bed I would always think about what I would do if I knew who my parents were. My thoughts were interrupted by Mr.Pinto, who came to tell us all a bedtime story.

Upon seeing Mr.Pinto, I was delighted. I felt blessed as he was a person whom I could always approach with any of my problems. He would like a magician solve all of them.

One day, I gathered the courage to approach Mrs.Pinto, who was sitting in the living room.

I went and asked her, "Mrs.Pinto, Can I ask you something?"

Mrs.Pinto frawned but said, "Make it quick."

"Do you know who my parents were?"

Mrs.Pinto angrily stared into my soul and said, "This is the last time I am hearing this nonsense, understood. I have taken you into my care this is what you have to keep in mind. From now on, you will not utter a single word about this topic."

Aarav, a boy from the orphanage heard it. He was of my age and my friend. We both shared our joys and sorrows. Aarav told me that approaching her was like putting my hand into a lion's mouth. However, he praised me for my courage. I came to know that Mrs.Pinto was not only strict but also hated anyone asking unnecessary questions. She followed the policy of her way or no way.

At that moment, Mrs.Pinto heard us. I was punished for staying awake past our bedtime. She dragged me out of our bedroom by my collar and ordered me to clean her store room. It was a dark room with little ventilation. I felt as if it wasn't cleaned since years. Many stuffs like old clothes, books, storybooks, pairs of shoes etc. were dumped in that room. Mrs.Pinto used to keep the stuffs in the store room locked and would give us something when she felt we were in desperate need of it. During my time cleaning the store room, I decided to stop thinking of having parents and be grateful for the life I was living. I decided to accept the fact that I was lucky to even survive. Soon, at midnight after cleaning for the whole day when I was about to go to sleep, Mr.Pinto entered, after Mrs.Pinto went to sleep. He felt guilty when he saw me in a miserable state. He had brought me some water and food. It took me two days to clean the storeroom. Time passed by pretty easily as Mr.Pinto would be there with me at midnight. He would fetch water and food for me. He even hummed me a lullaby so I could fall asleep. After I would go off to sleep, he would lock the door from outside so that Mrs.Pinto is unaware of him coming here.

I was also forced to work an hour extra, unlike my fellow friends. Being silent for long was tough for someone like me who was always eager to talk. When I approached Mr.Pinto, he told me to be grateful for what I have rather than concentrating on the negative aspects of life.

Soon, I began to find inner strength and a sense of gratitude for the small blessings in my life. Rather than dwelling on the negative aspects of my upbringing, I chose to focus on the positive side of life as well as hoping for a better life.

Few years had passed, and I learnt not to talk unnecessarily. I loved staying alone. I realized that if I didn't make any mistakes, neither me nor Mr.Pinto would fall into trouble. Furthermore, at the back of my mind, I was planning to escape and search for my parents. I was looking for a mother's tender love and a father whose strong shoulder would protect me. This feeling was getting deep rooted into my heart as if henceforth I wouldn't be able to live without it. It was a plan that I didn't tell anyone about as I didn't find it necessary. But later I mentally prepared myself that this was my home and that the other children in the orphanage were my family, along with Mr. and Mrs.Pinto. I decided that running away was not an option as Mr.Pinto was always there for me during my hard times, and it did not feel right to leave Mr.Pinto without repaying his kindness.

CHAPTER TWO

Seven Years on Planet Earth

Everybody feels extra special on one day out of three hundred and sixty-five days - their birthday. Young children's parents take their children and friends out and host a birthday party for them. I saw it in the orphanage when children used to host their birthday parties with us and their parents would give us gifts and food.

Upon seeing this, I always wished I had parents who would take care of me, buy me delicious sweets and cookies, and celebrate the day I was born. However, I thought that my parents had little regard for me so they left me when I was so small. Despite my countless prayers to the Almighty to help me to meet my parents at least once and spend my birthday with them, it never happened.

My thoughts were interrupted by the screeching voice of Mrs.Pinto. "Wake up, everyone," she spoke. I turned over to check the time and realized that it was only half past five, and there was still time before the wake-up call. Despite that, I decided to wake up and go downstairs as I didn't want to face beating from Mrs.Pinto. She addressed all the kids in the orphanage with a grin on her face. "Mr.Pinto has gone out for work, and hence you all will be under my scrutiny. Mistakes will not be excused, and serious action will be taken."

Every child in the orphanage understood that we were all in danger. The fact that no one remembered my birthday made me depressed. However, I was even more dejected as Mr.Pinto was not there. Without him, the cheerful orphanage would turn into a graveyard. The day started. All the kids were divided into groups.
As I was mowing the lawn, I noticed Mrs.Pinto grabbing Aarav by his collar and threatening to put him in a dark room. Seeing my best friend in trouble, I tried to request Mrs.Pinto to leave him and forgive him. However, the situation took a serious turn when she dragged both of us into the darkroom. She scolded both of us and we were punished to skip lunch. After two hours, She came to open the door of the dark room. I was told not to interfere in grown-ups business. She then turned to Aarav and warned him that this was the last time she has spared him. She allowed us out of the dark room. Slowly, the day turned to night as we worked continuously. After a day of hard work, we were allowed to go and rest. I was lost in thought about how my birthday turned into a mishap. I was disappointed because no one seemed to know my birthday until Aarav unexpectedly gave me a "Happy Birthday" message. "I was waiting to give you this note since morning," he said.

I was overjoyed. This was the first time I had ever received a note. I couldn't believe my eyes. Aarav thanked me for standing up for him and that he would never forget my birthday. This was the first time I had heard these delightful words. I was relieved to hear that there was someone who genuinely cared about me, even though my entire day had been a blunder. I thought it was a good day in my life as someone had given me a gift.

At night, Aarav surprised me by sharing a packet of cookies that Aarav had stolen from Mrs.Pinto's kitchen along with some imported chocolates. I had never tasted any imported chocolate before. I realised it was for this reason Mrs.Pinto was scolding him earlier. I thanked Aarav for being so thoughtful in remembering and celebrating my birthday. We both were delighted as we had each other.

I was extremely happy. I never had someone to celebrate my birthday until now. I expressed my gratitude to God for fulfilling my wish to be able to celebrate my birthday .

Emotional Turmoil

Awaiting the presence of Mr.Pinto was pretty exciting, we were all talking about the various sweets, clothes, and gifts he would bring for us. We were all overjoyed and excited. We came to know from Mrs.Pinto that he had gone for a week. We were waiting to see Mr.Pinto we started counting days for him to come. A week went by, and it was time for Mr.Pinto's arrival. The orphanage was cleaned, the lawn was mowed, and the dishes were washed. We also made an effort to clean our cupboard which was always a mess. As this one cupboard was shared by all the children in our orphanage. So, how much ever we try to arrange the cupboard it would always turn into a dumping yard. Everyone was desperate for Mr.Pinto's arrival.

Finally, the day arrived when Mr.Pinto was going to return to the orphanage. Aarav was so happy that he could not control his excitement and bolted outside the orphanage to welcome Mr.Pinto. Mrs.Pinto angrily glared at Aarav and screamt at the top of her lungs, "Get back in here!" Aarav, on the other hand, didn't bother.

After this act of bravery, Mrs.Pinto stood up and dragged him inside the orphanage by his ear. After that,

Aarav had to face terrible consequences. Not only was his school day to learn from teachers who had come to teach us got cancelled but he was also penalized to wash all the soiled utensils alone.

Mrs.Pinto was already in a terrible mood, so I decided to warn everyone to focus only on the chores assigned by Mrs.Pinto. I also informed everyone that Mr.Pinto was on his way and that we would all be free from Mrs.Pinto's control once he arrives. Everyone was suddenly enthusiastic after my speech.

However, I felt something wasn't right. Mr.Pinto had gone to many business meetings. Even after his busy schedule, he would always pamper me and promise to buy various goodies, toys, and new clothes before going. This time it was different. He had even refused to tell me where he was going. For some reason, I felt that something was about to happen to him. Suddenly, an odd sensation crept into my heart. Mr.Pinto and Aarav were my only family. I couldn't think of losing them.

Mr.Pinto was like a father figure to me, and I aspired to be like him. He had a huge impact on all the kids in the orphanage. I was worried about him. I was snapped out of my reveries by Mrs.Pinto's horrendous voice. She screamt, "Stop daydreaming and move your hands faster. It is already noon, and you haven't cooked lunch yet." In my mind, I cursed Mrs.Pinto. However, my anger was soon extinguished upon seeing Aarav. He started helping me in kitchen to prepare lunch. While chopping vegetables he started talking to me. "Look at your face, even God would be confused about what you are thinking. You barely smile, and when you talk, you don't have any facial expressions. It feels like you have no motivation in life. Even though humans are warm-blooded creatures, you look pale. It feels like you are passing each day of your life without fully living it." Soon, Aarav was again sent to clean the washroom.

Aarav, unlike any other person I had ever met, spoke on infinite topics. He was full of life. Hearing Aarav speak reminded me of the famous African quote: "He who talks too much ends up talking nonsense." After talking to him I felt he spoke on too many topics together but today what he spoke made sense to me. Soon, day turned to night. All the kids in the orphanage were tired after a long day of hard work, especially Aarav, who had not eaten anything since morning. Soon, everyone had forgotten about Mr.Pinto's arrival. Children were exhausted, they slept in no time. However, I was filled with anxiety.

My worry vanished when I heard the sound of Mr.Pinto's car. I was so excited that I woke everyone up. I told them that Mr.Pinto had returned. We all jumped out of our beds and went downstairs. Luckily, Mrs.Pinto was fast asleep after having a bottle of wine. We all waited eagerly at the front gate, and soon the person we all waited for had arrived. It was none other than Mr.Pinto. As soon as he entered, we all jumped towards him to hug him. In the process, poor Mr.Pinto slipped and fell. However, we all helped him up, and he was delighted to see us. We told him all that we had done in his absence. He would give all of us a patient hearing.

He gave us new toys he had purchased for us and some sweets for each of us. After all the love and affection showered on us, everyone retired to their beds.

Mr.Pinto stopped me and said, "I am glad you took care of everyone. You know when you are there, I know everyone will be happy. You know why I gave you the name 'Arabella' as 'you are god's gift to me'. You came into my life when I lost my child in an accident. I was driving the car and she was with me. All of a sudden, a truck appeared right in front of the windscreen. I had to apply the brakes instantly. I tried to stop the car but the car dashed against the truck. I got slightly hurt, but I lost my child. I have always thought that all children living here are the blessings of God. I see my child in each one of you. Mrs.Pinto wasn't that much bad either. She started hating kids from that day as she can't forget her child looking at all of you. She feels I am responsible for her child's death as I was the one who was driving. Forget her forgiving me, I have the guilt that I am responsible for my child's death. I always felt that god has sent you to me the next day after my child's death. So that I can bear the loss of my child. You have extra special place in my heart. I did not get any gift for you as I wanted to give you my most prized possession. It is my watch. It was given to me by my father, and I hope you will take care of it."

I was both surprised and happy as I had never expected Mr.Pinto to give me his watch. After talking to Mr.Pinto for a while, I too retired to my bed. I was happy that Mr.Pinto came back safely.

Enlightenment

Having Mr.Pinto back made a great impact on everyone. It didn't change the fact that Mrs.Pinto still made us work endlessly, but we were at peace, as someone who love us from the bottom of his heart is around us. A new wave of positive vibes flowed through our bodies; we felt a fresh surge of good energy.

In addition, some of the orphans would be extremely fortunate because some couples would be adopting children from our orphanage the following day. Unlike others, I was not excited as I was already thirteen years old. Most parents were reluctant to adopt a thirteen-year-old kid as they believed that they would not be able to mould a kid who would be too old to accept them as parents. I knew my chances of getting adopted were very slim.

Despite this fact, I knew I was not going to be adopted. I was happy for others though I always felt lonely from within and was desperate for a family. My thoughts were interrupted when Mrs.Pinto called me to the living room. She said, "Here is the list of some stuffs I have ordered. Go and get it. Take the money from Uncle Pinto. Now off you go."

So, I took the long list of groceries in my hand and asked Mr.Pinto for some money. After that, I went and bought the groceries from the store next to our building in the campus of our orphanage. It was a small room built and was given on rent to a shopkeeper by Mrs.Pinto so that she would get some extra income to spend on herself. It was in a corner of our playground, making our ground even smaller. I was asked to work in the kitchen. Everything was the same for me and the day ended just like it always did.

Early in the morning, we had three couples coming to adopt kids from the orphanage. Soon, dawn turned to dusk and two of our orphanage's children found loving homes.

As the day was getting over, a couple arrived. I knew that they would not select me, so I decided to continue cleaning the dinning table. Upon seeing me, they spoke to eachother for a while and requested Mr.Pinto to adopt me. I could not believe my ears. They said, "We always wanted to adopt an older kid.We would love to adopt you, will you stay with us?"

I was filled with happiness. My heart was overflowing with joy. They immediately spoke to Mrs.Pinto too. After a long conversation, I was told that I had to pack my bags in the morning.

After they left, I realized that it was my last day at the orphanage. It even struck me that I wouldn't be able to see Mr.Pinto and Aarav again. The thought of leaving them petrified me. Upon realizing this, I immediately ran to Mr.Pinto and I started sobbing on his lap. Even his eyes turned moist. He hugged me and said, "Even though I love you from the bottom of my heart, you have to go. I would never be able to take care of you as they will.

I want you to go with them with a free mind. Make an effort to speak to them, and understand them. They will take good care of you. Once you grow from a child into a fine young lady, come back and meet me. Until then, work on improving yourself. Go to bed now. It is a big day for you tomorrow."

I knew that Mr.Pinto was right, and I should not go on arguing about it. After all, I was getting what I was longing for. A new chapter in my life would begin from tomorrow. A chapter in which I would be able to feel and experience the love and affection of parents - something which I always wanted.

CHAPTER FIVE

A New Beginning

That night, I was barely able to get some sleep, as I was overjoyed by the fact that I was finally going to have parents. Over time, I had heard about kids going out with their parents, having food with them and sometimes even being cocky with them. I wanted to do all these things with my new parents.

Despite all the harsh conditions in which we were staying, whatever punishment we faced at the orphanage by Mrs.Pinto it was my home for the past thirteen years. My father figure Mr.Pinto, my friends in the orphanage who practically became my family and the punishments of Mrs.Pinto were all part of my life here. I was leaving it all now. My heart was filled with joy as well as grief.

All the memories flooded in front of me. I was lost into my thoughts. I was trying to digest the fact that I got what I wanted. I will be living the life with my parents. I was soon disturbed by the voice of Mrs.Pinto.

She shouted," Get up, and pack your bag."

I obeyed her orders like always and decided to pack. I packed all my clothes and few other items in one suitcase and headed downstairs for breakfast.

Mr.Pinto had made for all of us sandwiches along with milk as our breakfast. In my mind, I knew that Mr.Pinto could not afford such an extravagant meal. When I asked him about it, he said," I have done this as the kids who are leaving the orphanage will never return. This lavish meal is to treat them, as well as to lift the spirits of the ones who were not adopted this year."

I smirked and sat at the table. Mrs.Pinto who never was in a good mood was happy too and allowed all of us to sit and talk with each other, as from the next day, she would not see us.

After a good breakfast, Mr.Pinto addressed all the kids who were leaving the orphanage. He said, "I have always loved you all and I will miss your presence in the orphanage. However, you are now departing from the orphanage and are going to live life with your family. But keep in mind that I will always be there for you. I hope you all will love your parents. Do not trouble them and live the life which you always wanted to live with your parents. This is a new chapter of your life. I want you to enjoy every bit of it."

After Mr.Pinto's emotional speech, we all hugged him for the last time. Before we parted ways, I hugged all my friends in the orphanage. I then just looked at the whole orphanage once again, knowing that I would never be coming back again.

Before leaving, I met Aarav. I hugged him tightly knowing I would never see him again. I told Aarav, "I will never forget you and you will always be in my heart. I am happy to grow with you in the orphanage. We have shared our joy, sorrows with each other here. I will never forget how you got yourself in trouble to celebrate my birthday. I hope you will get adopted by some lovely parents who will shower blessings and love on you and will cherish you for life."

Aarav then hugged me, while tears rolled down our eyes.

Aarav spoke with a quavering voice, "I will miss you too."

With that we said our farewells. Soon, my new parents came to take me. I sat in their car, and I waved goodbye to all my friends and Mr.Pinto. I was really happy and excited to start a new journey in my life.

My parents introduced themselves as Mr. and Mrs.Wadia. Soon, they started to converse with me. I too introduced myself as Arabella. They asked what I did when I was in the orphanage and in which school did I go to. I came to know that they were both doctors. Hence, they would be mostly out. However, Mrs.Wadia was willing to give up her job to look after me. I told her it was not necessary, as I could live independently. We had good conversation to know each other on our way to our house.

Soon, we reached home. It was a huge mansion. They had a huge garage on one side. They had built a garden for me to play on the other side. It had swings, slides, monkey bars and a trampoline. They had many animals in their private bungalow. They had a dog along with many hens and chickens. It had a nice backyard and beyond the backyard was a beach. This huge mansion had a swimming pool too. This place was like my dream home. I never imagined living in such a beautiful house. I was overjoyed to meet my new parents and live a new life along with them.

CHAPTER SIX

Comparisons

Soon, I heard Mrs.Wadia's voice," Arabella, please come to the dining room." I was confused. I rushed to the dining room. I thought I was doomed. I knew, I was going to be scolded and would be punished. My heart skipped a beat as I barely knew Mr. and Mrs.Wadia. However, things went uphill for me.

I was already fascinated about the fact that, I would be living in such a huge bungalow. Till yesterday, I was living in a shabby place. No one cared about me except Mr.Pinto. I thought I was dreaming. I had never seen a beach. I was mesmerized by the view. I felt that it was all a dream. I pinched myself extremely hard to make sure it wasn't a dream.

Mrs.Wadia had prepared a lovely dinner for me. She had prepared Chessy Nachos, Cheese garlic bread and Pasta. I was astonished by the lavish meal which was made especially for me. I could not believe my eyes. My mouth was watering. Till yesterday, I thought having a sandwich was luxurious and now I was presented with so much food. I had never tried any of these dishes.

Mr. and Mrs.Wadia asked me to pull up a chair and sit down for dinner. I was very excited. I gobbled up all the food in no time. Mrs.Wadia was delighted seeing me eat so happily. After dinner, Mrs.Wadia brought her special custard for me. I had never tasted anything so sweet and tasty. I could not believe the life I was living.

I felt like I was some kind of VIP to get such special treatment. I could say I was living life the king size. After dinner, Mr. and Mrs.Wadia told me that I would be going to school the next day. I would be going to "The School of Oxford."

I could not express my happiness in words. I was always passionate about learning. However, I had never got any formal education but learnt little from Mr.Pinto and from few teachers who came voluntarily to teach us in the orphanage. I always tried reading from the books donated by people as I loved learning new things every day. Mrs.Wadia then led me to my bedroom. It was a huge room with nice bed along with a study table... and a TV!!!!!

Mr.Wadia asked me,"Arabella, where are your other clothes?" I spoke softly, "In the orphanage every year we only got three pairs of clothes that too, were worn and used. "Listening to this, next day he got dozens of clothes from a nearby mall.

Mrs.Wadia handed me my schoolbooks which I kept in the cupboard above my study table. I had never worn a uniform in my life. My school dress even had a blazer to wear over it. I placed it on the first shelf of my wardrobe. Mr.Wadia had got so many t-shirts, bottoms, dresses and night dresses. I felt he has purchased full store for me. I had never seen or worn such beautiful clothes in my life. I could see T-shirts of so many different colours - blue, black, white, red, purple etc., bottoms of different colours and dresses of different styles. With the help of Mr. And Mrs.Wadia I arranged all the dresses in a pile and placed it in the drawer of my wardrobe. On the hanger, we hung all my t-shirts. On the shelf below, we arranged my bottoms. I couldn't believe my eyes.

I was joyous. Earlier, I used to sleep on the old bed with bedbugs, along with all the kids at the orphanage in a room. Now, I have my personal bedroom with a bed and comfy bed sheet with my name printed on it. They had also installed a bookshelf for me. It was filled with old classics - books written by Enid Blyton, Harry Potter, etc. .I had never seen so many books for me to read in my life. I was very happy.

Mr.Wadia had got a new cupboard in which he asked me to place my toys. It was so huge, I felt three clones of mine could fit in it. I had never owned a cupboard in the orphanage as I only had three pairs of clothes which I would get every year when people donated their old and used clothes to us. The same was with our slippers. We never had slippers according to the size of our feet. Now, I was the owner of so many things.

Mrs.Wadia in her sweet voice said, "Arabella you must be tired, go to bed." She then tucked me into bed. I asked her to sit besides me. She sat next to me and told me you can share anything to me. Memories of the orphanage flashed in front of me. I started comparing my life in the orphanage to the present life. I was treated like a princess in my family. Without saying I think she understood what I was feeling so she cuddled me.

Mrs.Wadia then said, "I feel sorry for your hard life, Arabella. We will never leave you. We are always there for you." We hugged each other. I thanked God for answering my prayers and prayed for all the kids in the orphanage to get such loving and caring parents soon. I slept in my new peach coloured night suit and a cosy blanket over me. I slept with my mother sleeping next to me.

CHAPTER SEVEN

The Lessons

The next day, I woke up completely energized and happy. After such a long time, I found myself smiling. Iimmediately jumped out of bed and went to the bathroom to freshen up.

Mrs.Wadia had bought for me a blue tiffin box and pink water bottle which she kept on the shelf above my study table so that as soon as I get up I can see them. I was waiting for a beautiful day at school excitedly.

While I was in the shower, I found myself travelling through my old memories: the hardships, the struggle, the happiness, the jealousy, and the sadness. All these emotions surged through my mind. However, now everything was fine. I had finally found parents who were taking great care of me.

I had received great privileges from them. The fact they decided to even adopt a teenager was amazing to me. I was showered with love, clothes, good food, a place to stay, and every other thing one could wish for.

I got ready for the day. I tucked in my shirt and put on my blazer. As soon as I came out, both Mr. and Mrs.Wadia wished me "Good Morning".

She then told me, "Wow! you look so pretty in your new uniform Arabella. Sit down, and I will get breakfast for you."

I thought I was dreaming. No one had ever served me breakfast in the orphanage. Here, I have a loving and caring mother to make breakfast for me.

Mr.Wadia then said, "Arabella, I hope you have got all your books. Mrs.Wadia has prepared your favourite snack and has filled your tiffin box to take for school. I will be dropping you off to school. Your classroom is '7 C'. I hope you have a great time at school."

Soon, Mrs.Wadia arrived with breakfast and a glass of chocolate milkshake for me. I had the mind-blowing breakfast which was prepared for me. Before leaving, Mrs.Wadia waved goodbye to me and kissed my forehead. It was a feeling I can't express.

I was extremely delighted. I always wanted to live a life with my parents, and finally, I was living it. It was like a dream come true for me. I wished Mrs.Wadia goodbye and left for school.

As I reached my new school campus, I was amazed to see such a huge campus. It had three gates. My school had two buildings dedicated to education, a huge canteen, a church, and a hostel. They even had a massive garden, a basketball court, a badminton court, a volleyball court, as well as a sports room with various facilities.

I got down from Mr.Wadia's car. I then managed to find my class. I felt that as soon as I would enter, everyone would welcome me with open arms. But I was greatly mistaken. As soon as I entered, I saw all my classmates having the time of their lives.

Nobody was bothered about me, or rather, I was still trying to process the information. My class was divided into two halves. Half of the class was of the studious kids who were busy studying, and the other half was rather opposite of the first half. A few of them were busy arm wrestling, and the others were busy fighting with each other.

Soon, the bell rang, and the whole class suddenly got seated. My new class teacher introduced herself as Mrs.Fernandes. She then called me and introduced me. She said, "This girl here is your classmate. Her name is Arabella. I want you all to be her friend and help her. She, unlike you all, has been adopted by Mr. and Mrs.Wadia. Mr. and Mrs.Wadia are beautiful souls as they have got this tender bundle of joy into their lives. So she is very special and you all have to take extra care of her."

I was happy that my teacher was making an effort to introduce me to the class, as well as the fact that she was appreciating my parents. However, things turned out pretty bad for me after it as the class bully, Derrick, started teasing me. He shouted "Arabella is born in a trash."

On my first day of school, I was bullied by all my classmates. They teased me about the fact of being an orphan. They teased me by saying I was so disgusting as my real parents dumped me like a used tissue paper.

I was so upset. My whole day was filled with lots of bullying. I was thinking about how well I was treated at the orphanage by my friends. Aarav and all the kids in the orphanage loved me. To the extent that, Aarav bothered to go that extra mile for me by stealing cookies and imported chocolates for my birthday. All the kids in the orphanage helped me and moulded me into who I am today. Here, everyone was calling me worthless piece of tissue paper. I was hating this moment of my life. I was sad. I missed my orphanage friends.

BORN
IN A
TRASH

CHAPTER EIGHT

The Aftermath

I expected to have a great school life but it was the opposite. I was expecting to meet new people. I would make lifelong friends, and most importantly, I would be able to overcome my past.

But I guess, when life gives you a bit of happiness, it also gives you a bit of sadness which we have to accept as a pinch of salt. I was disappointed. If I had been in the orphanage, I would never have been bothered by it. As Mr.Pinto and Aarav were always on my side. I would have accepted it as my destiny.

My life had turned topsy-turvy. Everything was different as I had found parents who loved me and thought the best for me. They took care of me as they would of their daughter. I didn't want to trouble them with my problems ever. But in school these bullies harassed mae in all possible ways.

While, I was lost in my thoughts, I didn't realize it was already lunchtime. During lunch, I was eating the lovely tiffin packed by my mother. While, I was relishing the yummy snack prepared by her, I was suddenly surrounded by Derrick's gang.

I was teased about being adopted. I was called a trash can, a liability, and an unwanted person on the earth. Moreover, I was teased about the lovely lunchbox packed by Mrs.Wadia.

I later realised that the majority of the kids in this school never brought a lunchbox. Rather they preferred to eat in the canteen to look cool. I was amazed by this as the canteen food was pretty expensive. I felt lucky that my mother had prepared delicious food for me with love.

My sadness was just accumulating as now the whole class joined Derrick and his gang. Among the students in the class, I felt like an outcast. No one was there to support me or talk to me. Finally, my terrible day in school was over.

After school, Derrick and his group surrounded me and started singing "You are a loser. You don't have real parents. Your real mother hated you." It all happened in the hallway so the whole school came to know about it. I was so embarrassed that I just ran off.

In the car, Mrs.Wadia asked me "How was your day in school?"

I lied to her and told her with a fake smile on my face " Mom, It was amazing". I lied to her even though I knew lying was bad. I did not want to trouble her.

As I reached home, I went to my bedroom and started sobbing . In the bedroom, I thought how great it would be if I had friends like Aarav in school. All these kids were nothing but bullies. After sometime I felt better.

When Mr Wadia came home, I pretended to be very happy in my new school. Together we all had dinner. I made up stories about having so many new friends and all the kids loving me.

After dinner, I told Mr. and Mrs.Wadia that I was sleepy and wanted to go to bed. They allowed me. However, I couldn't fall asleep as many thoughts were going on .

I remembered my days in the orphanage where Aarav had fallen into trouble for me to get a packet of cookies and imported chocolates. I could never possibly forget the love and gratitude I had for the kids in the orphanage.

I was hurt when they spoke bad things about Mr. and Mrs.Wadia. For me, they were equivalent to God. They gave me a whole new life which I would have never been able to receive in the orphanage.

They provided countless numbers of clothes and toys, above all their love for me was incredible. I was awake till midnight when suddenly I felt drowsy, my eyes closed, and I fell asleep. You must be wondering that how often I am thinking of getting clothes, toys etc. but for a person who has seen scarcity, values the privileges given to them by God.

ORPHANAGE

CHAPTER NINE

A New Expereience

The following day, I went to school with zero motivation. I was frustrated that I had to see Derrick's face for five days a week.

As soon as, our class teacher Mrs.Fernandes arrived, she said, "Good Morning, class. I have some very exciting news. Our class will be going for a school educational tour after a week at Gir Forest in Gujarat. As most of you know it is a wildlife sanctuary and national park that is famous for being the natural habitat of the Asiatic lions. I am pleased to announce that we all will be going there for our educational trip this year. These are the registration forms. Please give them to your parents. "

I was suddenly filled with joy and excitement as I would be going out for the first time in my life. I had never stepped out of the orphanage and now I was going to Gujarat. I was so excited. I would be seeing so many animals like lions, deer, peacocks etc. I had never even imagined that I would be getting the opportunity to go there.

I had only seen places and animals in books but now I was getting the opportunity to see various animals and places in real life. I was amazed by this incredible luck. I thanked God for answering my prayer. Who could have imagined that, I would be adopted by such lovely parents who loved and cared about a teenage child? Not in my wildest dream would I think of possessing various toys, books, and clothes. My Mom will prepare tasty food for me. My Dad would play with me. Now, I would be going to Gir Forest. I felt as if a magician called God had transported me to a new world with his magic spell.

As soon as, I opened the form, I saw that one had to pay 25000 rupees to go to Gir Forest. My excitement suddenly turned into sadness. I knew that, it was not right to trouble Mr. and Mrs.Wadia. They already bought me so many new gifts and took utmost care of me.

It would be wrong on my part to take their love and care for granted. It was pretty expensive, and I did not want to be a brat who would not acknowledge their love and the amount of money they had spent on me. In the orphanage, we had never seen 25,000 rupees together.

While I was thinking to myself, I was disturbed by the sudden commotion in the class. Everyone was talking about going on the field trip, what would they wear and what would they do over there.

I was sad as I knew my parent's money was something that I would never take for granted. Soon, Mrs.Fernandes reminded us to show the form to our parents. If we were not going, then we had to bring a letter.

My plan to not show the form to my parents had failed. I thought that, if I did not show the form to my parents then they would not know about it and that I would not trouble them any further with my demands.

Soon, school was about to end, and luckily Derrick was absent, so I didn't have to see his face today. Till the time I reached home, I was contemplating whether or not should I show this form to my parents. I did not want them to think that I was a brat, but I knew that if I didn't show them the form, they would be sad that I wasn't open to share things with them. Nevertheless, I made up my mind to show them the form.

As I reached home, I handed over the form to Mrs.Wadia so that she could look at it. It was a Friday night. Mr.Wadia was at home. I told him too to have a glance at the form.

Mr. and Mrs.Wadia were delighted. They told me that they would help me with packing. Mr.Wadia instantly got the money out. They told me tomorrow in the afternoon after lunch, they would take me shopping to buy a new suitcase for me to pack all my luggage and all the other necessary items.

I was amazed to think they were willing to pay 25000 rupees for a five-day educational trip just for me. I was delighted to see that I was blessed with such great parents who prioritized my happiness over money.

Mr.Wadia told me "Arabella, I hope you have a great time over there. Don't forget to have lots of fun. Make sure to click many pictures so that we can frame them as memories."

After lunch, Mr. and Mrs.Wadia took me to the mall. It was my first time entering into one. It was a huge five storey building with many shops and a food court selling various food items.

I was amazed to see the fully air-conditioned mall with a huge number of shops with all kinds of things. My parents took me to the baggage section. They asked me to pick any bag I wanted.

I had never seen so many bags on display ever in my life. I was shocked to see bags of various designs and colours. I later chose a nice white bag with designs of orange, pink and green on it. Then Mrs.Wadia took me to the winter clothing section. There she made me try a few jackets till we found a perfect size for me. She then showed me sweaters of various colours. I chose a purple sweater.

When I showed it to Mr.Wadia he loved it. Over there Mr. and Mrs.Wadia helped me pick few clothes for me to wear on the trip. They bought all these things for me with a smile. After having dinner in the mall we came back to our house. After that, I neatly arranged all my clothes, sports shoes, and flip-flops in my new suitcase, along with some other accessories like hair bands, comb etc. I was so excited.

Mr.Wadia handed me the form along with the money for the trip. It all felt like a dream come true for me. I had such lovely parents who put so much effort for me. I truly thanked God for giving me such wonderful parents.

SHOES
CLOTHES

Realization

A week passed and the day I had to leave for educational trip had come. I was filled with excitement as I was now going on my very first trip. I woke up bright and early, filled with energy. I was surprised to see that Mr. and Mrs.Wadia were already awake. It was Sunday when I had to leave for my school picnic to the Gir Forest.

When I asked Mr. and Mrs.Wadia " Mom and Pops why did you wake up so early?" Mr.Wadia replied, "Our darling daughter is going on her first school trip. Of course, we would wake up early to make sure you have everything you need."

I was pleased to hear such sweet words from Mr.Wadia, but I knew they were sad as I would be going for five days. I could see him choked and unable to utter a word. I told Mr.Wadia, "Pops, you're pretty bad at lying. Just accept it you will miss me. Don't worry, I'll be back in five days. Instead of missing me, you and Mom can go out and enjoy."

Mr.Wadia was trying to control his emotions and then hugged me. That moment I felt that I should come back home soon. It was a feeling I could not describe like a feeling of home, knowing someone was awaiting my return. I promised Mr.Wadia I would come back as soon as possible.

I then turned towards Mrs.Wadia, who looked pale. I kissed her on her cheeks and said to her "Mom, I will miss you. I would be back soon." With tears in their eyes, they bid me goodbye.

I was sad to leave them. However, I was pretty excited too. This was my first ever school trip or rather my first trip anywhere. Excitement filled my heart. After my class teacher took the attendance, she divided the whole class into pairs of twos or threes.

Unfortunately, I was paired with Derrick and one more girl. I could not believe my luck. I tried to request the teacher to pair me with someone else, but she refused. Throughout the train ride, Derrick badmouthed me and continuously spoke ill about my parents.

I ignored him. I was frustrated with him, but I needed to stay calm as being angry wouldn't help. The next day, we arrived at Gir Forest. I was amazed to see a place filled with so much of greenery. I could hear the birds chirping and see butterflies sucking nectar from flowers.

Our class teacher then took us to our campsite. She took us to our tents. Our tents were made up of green cloth. It had a bed on the floor and little space kept for our belongings.

My class teacher said, "Your names are written on the tents so settle down in your respective tents. "Excitedly, the children ran to check their names written on the tents.

Mrs.Fernandes said, "We would be staying for the next four days in these tents. Keep the tents clean we may have a surprise check anytime."

I was upset when I saw that Derrick and I had our tents next to each other. After we all settled down in our tents, we were given a day off to rest as we had travelled so much and our teacher wanted us to get accustomed to the cold and dry weather at Gir.

From my tent, I saw that Derrick was lying down. He didn't seem to look well. I could see that he was shivering. I rushed to his tent to check on him. When I felt his forehead, I realized he had fever. But we were in the middle of a forest, so there was no medical facility.

I then removed my handkerchief, wet it with a little water, and placed it on his forehead. I opened my luggage and found some medicines that Mrs.Wadia had packed for me in case of emergency. I called the teacher and asked her to give him the medicine. Mrs.Fernandes did so. He went off to sleep. I kept my tent open so that I could keep an eye on him. After a while, when I went to see him, he had recovered. I thought he would thank me. Instead of thanking me, he said, "There was no need for you to enter my tent. I could manage everything by myself." My face turned red with anger, I stormed out of his tent regretting that I had taken care of him despite his bullying. We all rested a little and got acquainted with the surroundings. I got engrossed in the greenery around me.

Once my anger cooled, I sat on my bed and took out a book to read. Soon, it was dinner time. I went out, leaving Derrick in his tent. The food was delicious. After dinner, the tour guide told us we would have to wake up early at 6 a.m. Then we all went back to our respective tents.

I didn't say a word to Derrick and dozed off. Next day, I woke up early at 5:00 a.m. and got ready, planning to leave Derrick alone in the tent. I sat on a log and admired the scenery, getting some peace of mind. Nature always calms me down. It fills my heart with tranquility.

I was ready by 5:45 a.m. but Derrick had not woken up yet. I decided not to wake him and let him face the consequences.

However, I couldn't bear the thought of him getting into trouble and decided to wake him up. I shook him awake. Surprisingly, he didn't tease me. Instead he thanked me for waking him up on time. I was surprised by such a sudden change in his behaviour.

Maybe, he wasn't rude as I thought he was. After that, we all assembled early in the morning and along with our tour guide went trekking. During our trek, we saw many birds like yellow- crowned woodpecker, Indian vulture, Black- headed Oriole etc.

Finally, we stopped. It had been a long trek. During our break, we were handed some sandwiches and tea for breakfast. After that short and refreshing break, our tour guide set up a challenge between all our groups.

In the evening, we were taken to a field with various obstacle courses. There were prizes for the winners. Soon, the competitive spirit rose in everyone. We were tied to harnesses to prevent us from falling. Derrick and I were in the same team. As soon as, the guide blew his whistle, we bolted towards the obstacle course.

Derrick and I were in the lead. We quickly passed through the chain of tyres and crossed the bridge, surpassing our classmates. We both easily climbed the rock wall. The only thing left was to complete the last obstacle, the yellow commando net.

When we were almost at the top, Derrick slipped and fell. Luckily, he was safe because he was tied to the harness. I jumped down too and asked if he was okay.

After a couple of seconds, he calmed down, and together we climbed the wall again with a smile. Even though we came last we were okay with it. I felt we had established a good friendship.

I suddenly felt that, Derrick and I made a good team. After that, when we rested in our respective tents. I started changing my clothes as I smelled like a pig by the end of the day. After having a bath and changing into a night suit, I cleared the mess in the tent. We had dinner and I fell asleep in a jiffy.

Derrick approached me suddenly the next morning while I was getting ready for the day. At first, I thought he wanted to pester me, but instead, he asked if I knew how to put his clothes into a bag, and to select which T-shirt to wear. He had his bed covered with his red T-shirt, yellow T-shirt, blue hoodie etc. He emptied his full suitcase. His tent was in a mess. I went to him and helped him tidy it up. He then asked me to teach him to fold the clothes as he had never even folded a handkerchief. I was surprised because in the orphanage, everyone even washed their clothes from a very young age. Nevertheless, I decided to help him since we were in the same team for the next two days. I taught him how to fold the clothes and arrange them in bags.

After that, he thanked me. I was still shocked that the guy who bullied me every day at school was now trying to be a good classmate. I was confused at first, but then I thanked God for placing me and Derrick in the same group as I felt we got to know each other better.

I was delighted to see that Derrick asked me for help, as it was the first step to friendship. Finally, we became friends. I was extremely happy. We packed our stuff properly in our bags, with some laughter while we chatted with each other.

As always, the food was delicious. After a sumptuous meal, I returned to the tent. Seeing the messy tent, I started cleaning. Looking at me cleaning my tent, he started cleaning his tent too. We made our beds, folded our blankets neatly, and arranged our clothes in the cupboards. We read books in the afternoon and took a short nap. Soon, it was time for the evening safari. This time, we had jeeps to travel in as we were going deep into the forest to try to spot some Asiatic lions.

Our tour guide gave us instructions on how to proceed. We all ventured into the forest. After an hour and a half, we were deep in the forest. No one dared to utter a word. We were still trying to process the wonderful scenery around us.

Soon, our jeep spotted an Asiatic lion. We considered ourselves lucky. Our tour guide shared some information about Asiatic lions. After a little while, we saw a lioness with her cubs. It was an amazing sight. I realized even in animals parents take care of their offspring. This parental love is bliss.

I was delighted to see the outside world. I had only seen lions, tigers, and other animals in books, but now it was different. I could see them in real life along with my classmates.

When we returned to our campsite, everyone was talking about our jeep. This confused me. When I asked Derrick, he told me that we were the only jeep that saw Asiatic lions and a lioness. No one else had spotted them.

I was surprised and asked, "But we all went by the same route. Why didn't the others see them?"

He replied, "Lions and lionesses keep moving and hunting for their next prey. So, not everyone gets the chance to see them. You can consider us lucky."

We chatted with each other on some random topics. We sat on a log near our tent and gazed at the stars in the sky for a while. As time passed it became colder. We went to our tents and slept.

CHAPTER ELEVEN

Bonding

The next day was free for us to pack our belongings and enjoy each other's company. I spent the whole morning packing. After lunch, we all decided to explore the campsite.

With our class teacher's permission, we started exploring our surroundings. After some time, we found a beautiful lake. We sat there, had fun in the water and admired the view. In the evening, we returned to our campsite, as it was our last day at the camp.

Before leaving, we all collected wood to start a bonfire. For dinner, we had a huge barbeque in the open. After a nice dinner, we started a bonfire. We arranged a few logs and chairs for everyone to sit around the fire, as it got cold at night.

We chatted about our dreams and ambitions. Some of my classmates wanted to be doctors, engineers, and dentists, and a few wanted to be botanists. I had never seriously thought about my future, but the conversation led me to consider other professional fields. I had always been passionate about becoming a dentist. We then started sharing our pasts. Most of my classmates were wealthy and had great childhoods, yet they had complains about their parents of not buying them luxurious branded clothes and shoes instead bought them normal branded stuffs which they considered cheaper and uncool. I thought about how they had everything they wanted and yet were cribbing about brands. Our conversation was interrupted by our Tour Guide.

He said, "Since today is our last day of camp, my subordinates and I have checked all your tents. I am proud to announce that the winners of the cleanest tents are Derrick and Arabella."

We were both delighted. This was my first time winning anything. I held my head high with newfound confidence as Derrick and I were handed the trophies.

Suddenly, Derrick announced, "I would like to say a few words."

The Tour Guide said, "Sure Derrick, go ahead."

He started speaking "Until I came here. I felt I was the best. I used to bully many children as I always felt I was superior to all of them. When I came here I realised I was nobody. I couldn't even fold my handkerchief. On the other hand, I saw Arabella doing her work like a pro. I learnt everything from her. I realised that there are many children far better than me. I had even harassed Arabella. Yet she was kind enough to take care of me when I wasn't well. She helped me here whenever I was in need. In school, I had made her life miserable. In front of everyone, I was always teasing her. I would like to apologize to her in front of everyone."

I was surprised by Derrick's honesty. I couldn't gather words to say anything to Derrick. Somehow I could just say," It's ok. We are friends now."

The tour guide praised both of us- Derrick for his honesty and me for my hard work. He then asked me to give a speech about anything I liked or my thoughts which I would like to share with them.

I started by saying, "I heard everyone's conversation about their future ambitions. I enjoyed that, I got inspired by it but I didn't like how everyone was complaining about their parents, thinking poorly of them for buying a different brand of clothing. I feel one should respect their parents. I believe I have the right to say this, having experienced life both in an orphanage and with my new parents."

"Parents are the ones who listen to all our complaints and worries, help us to find solutions, and support us in our failures. They are the guiding light in our journey of life without whom we could never fulfil our dreams and ambitions. Everyone here wants to be doctors, engineers, and more. However, we shouldn't forget it's our parents who pay for our education without complaining and help us throughout our life to get what we want."

"From shoes to clothes and education, our parents provide everything to us. They work overtime just to buy us what we want. If one fails to realise what their parents do for them and does not respect them, then they are very selfish."

"In the orphanage, we don't have anyone to care about our silent tears. Trust me, no one can be as loving, compassionate, kind, and selfless as our parents. All our wants and desires are taken care of by our parents. Their life revolves around us."

"In the orphanage, we live at the mercy of others. Our basic needs are just managed. When we live with our parents, our fathers earn not for themselves, but to give us a better life. Our moms cook food for us, considering our dislikes and likes. They have forgotten themselves for us. Their struggles are forgotten when they see a smile on our faces. My mom sleeps after I sleep and wakes up before me to pack my water bottle and tiffin. Isn't that love?"

"My biological mother abandoned me at a very young age, leaving me in the orphanage like a used tissue paper. Maybe she had her reasons. I don't intend to know who she was. For me, my parents are Mr. and Mrs.Wadia, who saw me in the orphanage when I wasn't in the best clothes or nice haircut. Yet, they chose me. I believe I may not have been born in Mrs.Wadia's womb, but I was born in her heart."

Tears rolled down everyone's cheeks, including mine. While talking, I realised we should give unconditional love to our parents, who live their lives for us.

We came back from our great trip. As soon as I reached home, Mr. and Mrs.Wadia were waiting for me. They opened their arms wide and greeted me with huge hugs. I knew I had come back to the right place where my heart lies, which is my home. A home is not just a place with walls instead, it's a place that has countless memories of pain, joy and laughter...... all with our parents!

Now, in school all the classmates were my friends. Derrick and I had become the best of friends. The school's atmosphere had changed. Everyone was now willing to talk to me and they included me in their groups. Also, the teachers loved me and I started to love my school. I was not feeling like an outcast anymore.

Everything was falling into place in my life. I am living the life of a princess where my home is my kingdom. I loved this feeling of being at home with my parents. In the end, I can say my life's journey started from shadow and is leading towards sunshine...AND...MY LIFE'S JOURNEY CONTINUES.........

Epilogue

This book is not just a story about the protagonist named Arabella, a girl living in an orphanage who is mature beyond her years due to the life she has spent there. She evolves even more when she is adopted by a kind couple.

Through this book, I have attempted to navigate through the simple emotions of love, kindness, respect, and more, that we develop in our hearts. With the advent and proliferation of the internet, children are spending very little time with their parents, and therefore, natural conversations between them are diminishing. This is a relationship that we easily take for granted.

This book attempts to tap into our inner selves and ask ourselves whether this relationship is not worthy of taking it seriously and admiring the beauty of two selfless individuals who put their lives aside to live for us.

I hope this book can convey the important message of loving our parents to lead a happy and fulfilling life. The objective of this book isn't to preach but to highlight an aspect of life that deserves our attention.

Reviews And Ratings

Now that you have completed reading the book, I kindly request your valuable feedback. If this book has been able to connect with you emotionally, even for a moment, then it's my humble request to write a review. In this fast-evolving world, I feel we have left behind emotions and are living our lives like robots. This is a small initiative from my side to tap into our emotions.

For an author, there is no greater or better return than a testimonial.

Please feel free to write to avichalvritti@gmail.com.

Mobile : 9819988539

Acknowledgements

We cannot do everything ourselves. We all need people around us who support us and believe in us.

I thank from the bottom of my heart all the people mentioned below for supporting me, believing in me, and giving their precious time and advice so that I could give my best to this book. A very big thank you to all of you from the bottom of my heart!

I would like to thank these special people who have been my guiding force for this book:

My parents, teachers, the Principal of Villa Thereasa High School, Jaywant C Yadav (Assistant Session Judge Nagpur), Dr. Tinu Agrawal, Dr. Moujesh Agrawal, Smita Vora, Vishal Gupta, Mity Shah, Chirag Shah and friends.

A special thanks to my favourite teacher, Sohan Sir, for creating these beautiful illustrations and bringing Arabella to life.

Website: www.yellowcanvas.in

Disclaimer

Although the publisher and author have made every effort to ensure that the information in this book was correct at press time and while this publication is designed to provide accurate information about the subject matter covered, the publisher and author assume no responsibility for errors, inaccuracies, omissions, or any other inconsistencies herein and hereby disclaim any liability to any party for any loss, damage, or disruption caused by errors or omissions, whether such errors or omissions result from negligence, accident, or any other cause.

The ideas, procedures, and suggestions contained in this book are not intended as a substitute for consulting with an expert.

Neither the author nor the publisher shall be liable or responsible for any loss or damage allegedly arising from any information or suggestion in this book.

Names, characters and incidents in this book are either the products of the author's imagination or used in a fictitious manner.Any resemblances to an actual person, living or dead, or actual events is purely coincidental.